Merry Christmas
A Storybook Collection

Scholastic Inc.

New York   Toronto   London   Auckland   Sydney
Mexico City   New Delhi   Hong Kong   Buenos Aires

Once There Was a Christmas Tree
Copyright © 2005 by Jerry Smath.

Ten Timid Ghosts on a Christmas Night
Copyright © 2002 by Jennifer O'Connell.

Merry Christmas, Stinky Face
Text copyright © 2002 by Lisa McCourt.
Illustrations copyright © 2002 by Cyd Moore.

ISBN-13: 978-0-545-01341-3
ISBN-10: 0-545-01341-0

10 9 8 7 6 5 4 3 2   09 10 11

Printed in China
This collection first published October 2007

New Material Only	Matériaux neufs seulement
Reg. No. 04T-1654309	N° de permis 04T-1654309
Content:	Contenu:
Polyurethane Foam	Mousse de polyuréthane

Table of Contents

To: Olivia Rose Kearns – J.S.

Once There Was a
Christmas Tree

by Jerry Smath

"It's almost Christmas!" said Mrs. Bear. "And we still don't have a Christmas tree!"

"Don't worry," said her husband. "I'll find one."

Mr. Bear took his saw and went deep into the woods. There he found the biggest tree he could carry and brought it home.

Mr. Bear put the tree in the living room.

"It's a beautiful Christmas tree," said his wife. "But it's much too tall."

"I'll fix that!" said her husband.
With his saw, he cut the tree in half.

Just then Mrs. Bear looked out the window. She saw
Mr. Fox pulling his son on a sled. They were going into
the woods to look for a tree.

"Why don't we give them the top of our tree?" she said.
Mr. Bear agreed. So Mrs. Bear tied a big bow to the top
of the Christmas tree and took it outside.

"Yoo-hoo! Mr. Fox!" called Mrs. Bear.
"We took our tree and made it two.
One half for us, one half for you."
Mr. Fox was delighted. "Thank you so much," he said.
"What a wonderful present!"

Mr. Fox put the tree on the sled. Then he and his
son turned the sled around and pulled it home.

Once the tree was up, the two foxes stood back to admire it.

"It's the prettiest Christmas tree I've ever seen," said the little fox.

His father thought so, too.

They were just about to decorate their tree when Mr. Fox thought of his friend Old Rabbit.

"Old Rabbit lives all alone," he said. "And he doesn't have a tree this year."

"Our tree is big!" said his son. "Why don't we share it with him?"

"Good idea!" said Mr. Fox. So he took his saw and cut their tree in half.

Together Mr. Fox and his son took the top of their Christmas tree to Old Rabbit's house.

When Old Rabbit opened the door, Mr. Fox and his son said,
"We took our tree and made it two.
One half for us, one half for you."

Tears came to Old Rabbit's eyes when he saw their gift.
"How kind of you both," he said.

Old Rabbit brought the Christmas tree into his house and put it in his window.

Next, he put a silver star on top of the tree. Then, one by one, he added the ornaments.

Old Rabbit was almost done when . . . OOPS! One ornament that looked like a carrot bounced off the tree.

It kept rolling until it stopped by a hole in the floor.

"Thank goodness it didn't fall in!" said Old Rabbit. "That was my favorite one!"

Just as Old Rabbit was about to pick up the ornament, it was pulled into the hole.

Peeking down into the hole, he saw Mother Mouse and her three children. They were trying to eat the carrot ornament. "Don't eat that!" he shouted. "It's made of wood!"

Old Rabbit saw that the Mouse family was hungry.
So he invited them to dinner.

Afterwards, Old Rabbit and Mother Mouse
chatted and watched the children play.

"It's nice to have friends," said Old Rabbit, smiling.

It was getting late.

Mother Mouse carried her sleepy children home and tucked them into bed.

Old Rabbit went to bed, too, but he could not sleep.
When he looked at his pretty tree in the window, he
knew why.

"It's Christmas Eve!" he thought. "The Mouse family
should have a Christmas tree of their own!"

Old Rabbit went to the window and cut the top off his tree.

Quietly he tiptoed over to the hole and slipped the little tree into the Mouse family's room.

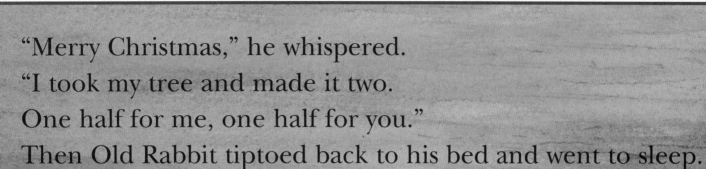

"Merry Christmas," he whispered.
"I took my tree and made it two.
One half for me, one half for you."
Then Old Rabbit tiptoed back to his bed and went to sleep.

Once there was a Christmas tree—

—but sharing made it four.

And Santa Claus left presents under every one.

For my mom and dad, Lee and Norman Barrett—
Remembering all of our Christmases together

Ten Timid Ghosts on a Christmas Night

by
Jennifer
O'Connell

1 One timid ghost on a Christmas night—
Waiting and watching by candlelight.
She heard a jingle in the dark outside
And rushed to the window—her eyes open wide.

2 Two timid ghosts on a Christmas night—
Waiting and watching by candlelight.
They looked outside and, up in the sky,
A team of reindeer was flying by.

3

Three timid ghosts on a Christmas night—
Waiting and watching by candlelight.
They heard a clatter and a "ho, ho, ho"
From up on the rooftop out in the snow.

4 Four timid ghosts on a Christmas night—
Waiting and watching by candlelight.
They saw a sleigh on the roof so high—
Shiny red in the snowy sky.

5 Five timid ghosts on a Christmas night—
Waiting and watching by candlelight.
They felt frosty air from the fireplace,
So they hid in the kitchen, just in case.

6 Six timid ghosts on a Christmas night—
Waiting and watching by candlelight.
They heard a *THUMP* in the living room
And peered down the hallway into the gloom.

7   Seven timid ghosts on a Christmas night—
Waiting and watching by candlelight.
They heard some rustling and a merry hum.
They crept in closer to see who had come.

8 Eight timid ghosts on a Christmas night—
Waiting and watching by candlelight.
They peeked round the corner
  and saw chocolates and fruits,
Peppermint candies . . . and big, black boots!

9 Nine timid ghosts on a Christmas night—
Waiting and watching by candlelight.
They spied ten stockings hung in a row
And someone in red by their tree all aglow!

10

Ten timid ghosts on a Christmas night—
Waiting and watching by candlelight.
They saw so many presents and, up at the top,
A bright, red hat going hippity-hop. . . .

One startled Santa on a Christmas night
Gave ten timid ghosts a great big fright!

"Hello!" said Santa. "There's no need to fear.
I've come to bring you some Christmas cheer!"

The ghosts opened gifts
On that cold winter's night,
Laughing with Santa
By the Christmas tree light.

And when it was time for Santa to go,
Up the chimney he went, out into the snow.
The ghosts waved good-bye as his sleigh took flight.
"Merry Christmas to all on this wonderful night!"

For that tiny creature who's already getting so many big-brother kisses through my belly button! ♡ ~L.M.

For Lisa, whose words always inspire happy images and many smiles! ♡ ~C.M.

Merry Christmas, Stinky Face

Written by Lisa McCourt ☺ Illustrated by Cyd Moore

Christmas was almost here. But I had a question.

Mama, what if the snow kept falling and falling so much that we couldn't open our door?

"I know what we'd do.
We'd crawl out of our
window into the snow
with some cups and juice.
We'd sit in front of our door
and have a giant snow-cone
party until we'd eaten up
all the snow!"

But, Mama, what if we finally opened the door ~ but then a big, wintry wind blew our Christmas tree away?

"If a wind did that, I would grab the coatrack from the hallway and decorate it with our brightest lights and ornaments. I'd put a star on the top, and we'd have a beautiful Christmas coatrack to sing our carols around."

But, Mama, but, Mama, what if I built a little snowman, and he followed me inside ... but our house was too warm and he started to **Melt?**

"It sounds like we'd have to set up a nice chilly room for him in the freezer. We'd give him peppermint ice cream for dinner and cover him with a blanket made of woven icicles so he'd stay frosty-cold all night long."

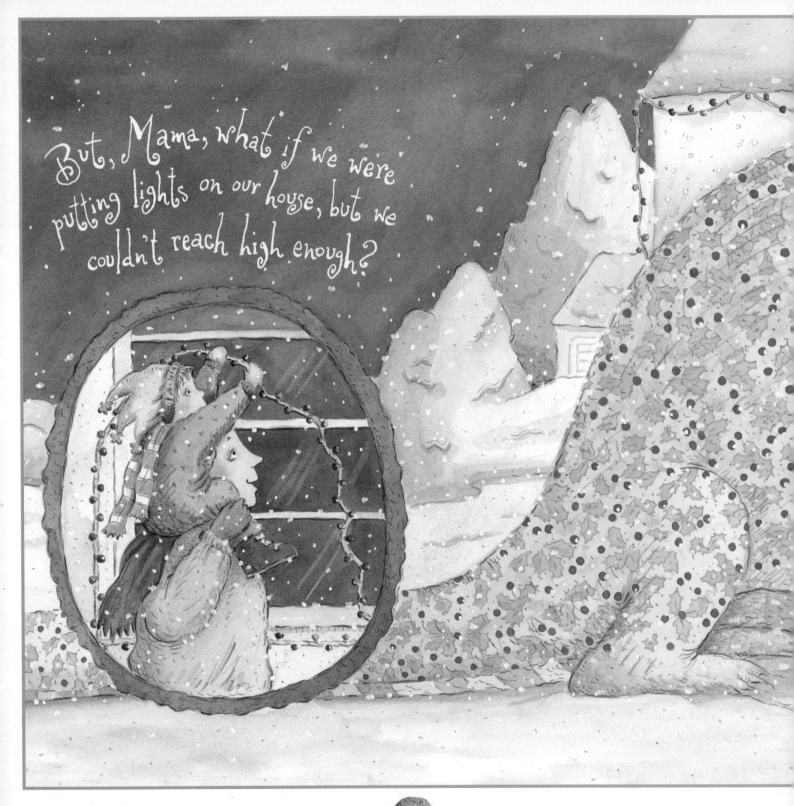

But, Mama, what if we were putting lights on our house, but we couldn't reach high enough?

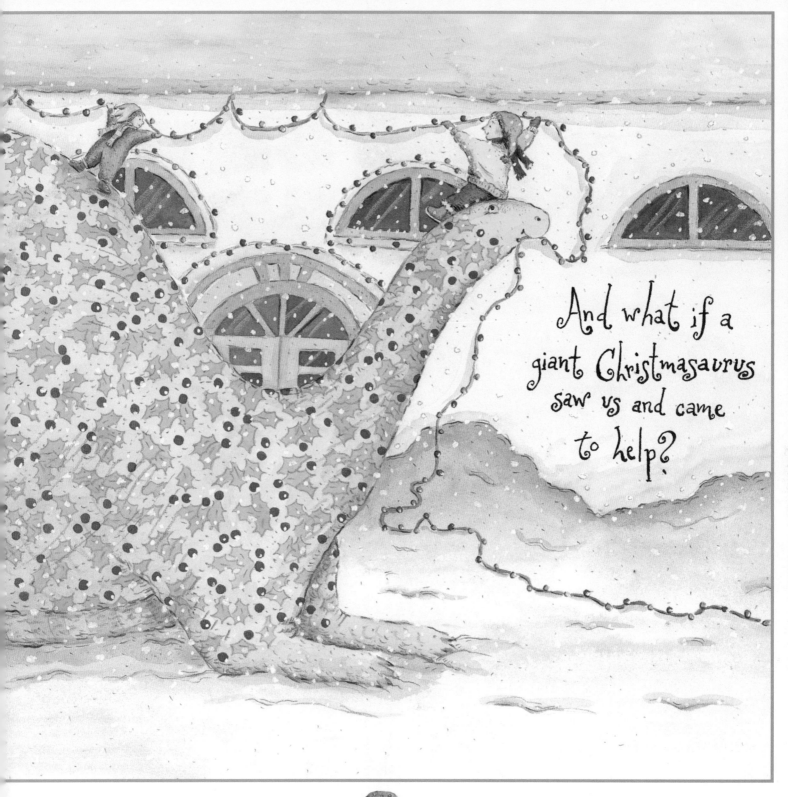

And what if a giant Christmasaurus saw us and came to help?

"Well, of course, if a Christmasaurus helped, we'd have to thank her with some Christmas cookies and hot cocoa."

Okay, Mama. But what if Santa landed on our roof, and one of his reindeer got his antlers stuck in the branches of the tree that hangs over my bedroom window?

"Oh, that would be a problem, wouldn't it? Maybe we should leave your saw here in case Santa needs it to cut any branches."

But, Mama, but, Mama, what if Santa's boot falls off while he's driving the sleigh,

and his foot is so cold that he tries to wear my
stocking on his foot ... but it doesn't fit?

"Hmmm. I guess we could leave these warm snow boots out with the saw—just in case."

But, Mama, but, Mama, what if Santa's lips get chapped from all that flying?

What if the sleigh needs a new coat of paint?

What if the sack of toys starts to rip?

What if the reindeer need their fur brushed?

"There! That should do it."

Merry Christmas, Mama!

"Merry Christmas, my Stinky Face."